SWEET PEAS AND HONEYBEES

Read the rest of the books in the
FRIENDSHIP GARDEN
series:

Green Thumbs-Up

Pumpkin Spice

Project Peep

And coming soon:

Starry Skies and Fireflies

the FRIENDSHIP garden

SWEET PEAS
AND
HONEYBEES

by Jenny Meyerhoff
illustrated by Éva Chatelain

ALADDIN
New York London Toronto Sydney New Delhi

ALADDIN

An imprint of Simon & Schuster Children's Publishing Division

1230 Avenue of the Americas, New York, New York 10020

First Aladdin paperback edition May 2016

Text copyright © 2016 by Simon & Schuster, Inc.

Illustrations copyright © 2016 by Éva Chatelain

Also available in an Aladdin hardcover edition.

All rights reserved, including the right of reproduction in whole or in part in any form.

ALADDIN is a trademark of Simon & Schuster, Inc., and related logo is a registered trademark of Simon & Schuster, Inc.

For information about special discounts for bulk purchases, please contact Simon & Schuster Special Sales at 1-866-506-1949 or business@simonandschuster.com.

The Simon & Schuster Speakers Bureau can bring authors to your live event. For more information or to book an event contact the Simon & Schuster Speakers Bureau at 1-866-248-3049 or visit our website at www.simonspeakers.com.

Book designed by Laura Lyn DiSiena

The text of this book was set in Century Expanded LT Std.

Manufactured in the United States of America 0416 OFF

10 9 8 7 6 5 4 3 2 1

Library of Congress Control Number 2016931716

ISBN 978-1-4814-3918-3 (hc)

ISBN 978-1-4814-3917-6 (pbk)

ISBN 978-1-4814-3919-0 (eBook)

SWEET PEAS AND HONEYBEES

CONTENTS

CHAPTER 1: S-U-M-M-E-R!   1

CHAPTER 2: Buzz Off!   11

CHAPTER 3: Anna to the Rescue!   29

CHAPTER 4: Bee-ing Brave   41

CHAPTER 5: Lemonade for Sale!   53

CHAPTER 6: *Mmmm,* Honey!   67

CHAPTER 7: The Big Bee Bash   85

CHAPTER 8: Sweet Endings   103

ACTIVITY: The Waggle Dance Game   116

RECIPE: Anna's Easy Honey Cinnamon Ice Cream   118

CHAPTER 1

S-U-M-M-E-R!

Little glimmers of sunlight sparkled in Anna Fincher's window, and one sunny beam warmed her cheek. Anna sat up in bed and smiled at the green leaves of the oak tree fluttering outside her bedroom window. She tilted her head and listened to the sweet coo of a mourning dove. There was only one word that could describe such a perfect day. S-U-M-M-E-R!

Anna hopped out of bed and got dressed in the special outfit she had laid out the night before. Shorts and a light T-shirt to keep herself cool, a wide-brimmed hat to keep the sun off her face, and thick socks with sturdy gardening boots. Anna couldn't wait to spend all day in the Friendship Garden.

During the school year, Anna and her friends visited the garden several times a week as part of an after-school gardening club. Now that it was summer, Anna's teacher, Mr. Hoffman, was leading a Friendship Garden summer program called Friends, Fun, and Flowers. For two whole weeks, Anna and her friends would get to hang out in the garden all day—well, not really all day, since there would be field trips and other activities in addition to gardening.

Anna hurried to the kitchen for breakfast.

"Good morning, Anna Banana!" Anna's father was already in the kitchen. He was the main cook at home, because Anna's mother was the head chef at a fancy restaurant. Mr. Fincher spooned a large dollop of yogurt into a blue bowl. "This morning I will be serving make-your-own yogurt bowls with homemade granola."

Anna took her bowl to the table and spooned sliced bananas, blueberries, granola, and a drizzle of honey onto her yogurt as Anna's mother shuffled into the kitchen in her pajamas. Anna's younger brother, Collin,

walked in behind her carrying a butterfly net and a magnifying glass. Collin swung the net around and then plunked it down, right on Anna's head.

"Gotcha!" he shouted.

Anna pulled the net from her hair. "I'm not a bug, Collin," she reminded him, even though that seemed obvious to her.

"I know," Collin said. "I was just practicing."

Anna took a deep breath and tried not to feel annoyed as Collin laid down his net. When everyone was at the table, Anna's mom wrapped both hands around her coffee mug and said, "Are you two ready for camp?"

Anna nodded as she licked yogurt and honey from the back of her spoon. "I can't wait! Maria gave the Friendship Garden an extra plot so we can grow rosebushes and fancy flowers!"

Collin looked at Anna's bowl, then added all the same toppings to his yogurt as Anna's. "I can't wait too," Collin said, taking in a mouthful of yogurt. He finished chewing, then added, "Bugs, Bugs, Bugs is going to be even better than first grade. The website said that a real entomologist was going to talk to us. That's a person who studies bugs!"

Collin wriggled his fingers, then crawled them up Anna's arm. A shiver ran down her spine. She knew bugs could be important for the garden, but she didn't like to get too close to them.

Anna liked her little brother, but some-times it seemed like all he thought about was bugs—and his favorite bug was *bugging* Anna. She was glad they would each be doing their own activity for the summer.

"I hope I find an Eastern Tiger Swallow-tail today!" Collin said.

Anna's parents gave each other a look, then her father sighed. "Collin, we have to tell you something that might be a little disappointing."

Collin tilted his head and looked at his father through the magnifying glass. "What?" he asked.

"We found out last night that not enough kids signed up for Bugs, Bugs, Bugs," Anna's mother said. "They had to cancel the class."

"But," Anna's father said, holding up one finger, "because bugs and gardens naturally go together, they've decided to combine the classes."

Anna's parents watched Collin's face with concerned expressions. "What do you think?" Anna's mom asked.

Collin took another bite of granola and shrugged while he chewed. "Okay," he finally said. "Sounds good. Now Anna and I can be partners if we need partners for something."

Anna's parents sat back in their chairs, both smiling with relief. "Anna's a great partner," said her father. "I'm glad you're not too disappointed."

Anna ate another bite of yogurt to hide her frown. Anna wasn't glad that Collin was joining her gardening class. And she wasn't glad that gardening had turned into gardening and bugs. She wanted to learn about marigolds and morning glories, not about creepy-crawlies. And she wanted to hang out with her friends, *not* with her brother. Suddenly Anna's perfect summer day felt a lot less perfect.

BUZZ OFF!

Anna's mood picked back up the moment she entered the Shoots and Leaves Community Garden. The sight of so many green plants bursting from the ground made her thumbs twitch with excitement. And the sound of four happy hens pecking in the dirt made her toes tingle with joy.

As Anna walked through Shoots and

Leaves, she waved at the other gardeners. Shoots and Leaves was a *community* garden. That meant people from all over Anna's neighborhood could rent a plot in the garden to plant their own flowers and vegetables. The Friendship Garden was the plot that belonged to Anna's school. It was the biggest plot, and it was all the way at the back of the garden.

Mr. Hoffman smiled at Anna as she and Collin followed the paths between the other plots all the way back to the Friendship Garden. Anna's friends and classmates Kaya and Reed were already there, along with a bunch of other kids. They were feeding the chickens that used to live in their classroom until Anna got the Friendship Garden to build a chicken coop as a birthday surprise for Kaya. Mr. Hoffman called the rest of the kids to join him, then asked them to sit on the edge of a raised wooden ledge that made the Friendship Garden's border.

"Welcome to Sweet Peas and Honeybees!" Mr. Hoffman said. "That's the name of our new class about gardening *and* insects. Some of you may know each other already, but let's introduce ourselves anyway. When it's your turn, please tell us your favorite vegetable and your favorite insect."

"What about flowers?" Anna asked. She didn't care about insects. She wanted Friends, Fun, and Flowers.

Mr. Hoffman gave her a smile. "Don't worry. Flowers will still be an important part of camp."

Anna looked around at the group as Mr. Hoffman called on different kids to say hello.

Besides Anna and her friends, there were four older boys who all wore baseball caps, two younger girls in matching pigtails, and two older girls, Simone and Imani. Anna already knew Simone and Imani since Simone's mother, Maria, was the president of Shoots and Leaves, and Imani was Simone's best friend.

When it was Anna's turn, she stood up and said, "Hi, I'm Anna, and my favorite vegetable is a sugar snap pea. My *least* favorite insect is an aphid because it eats tomato plants, but my favorite insect is a ladybug because it eats aphids."

Anna sat down and Collin stood up, clutching his magnifying glass in both hands. He seemed a little nervous, so Anna patted him on the shoulder.

"I'm Collin," he said quietly. "My favorite

vegetable is a carrot and I can't choose just one insect, so my favorite group of insects is Lepidoptera larvae. That means caterpillars. They are cool because they eat a lot and they can move like a wave and they all look really different."

Then Collin lay down on the ground and began to wiggle and squirm along the edge of the garden. "This is how caterpillars move," he said, sending a wave down his body.

"Collin, be careful!" Anna started to say, but it was too late. His foot had knocked over the watering can, and water splashed all over

Anna's boots. It didn't even matter that her boots were waterproof, because some of the water had splashed *inside* the boots and now Anna had wet socks. G-R-O-S-S!

Collin sat back down next to Anna. "Want me to teach you the caterpillar crawl when we get home?" he asked.

Anna pressed her lips together. She wanted dry socks. She wanted flowers. She didn't want anything to do with bugs.

When everyone was finished with their introductions, Mr. Hoffman made an announce-ment. "We are going to start out today with a really special field trip. We are going to visit my friend Mr. Blanco. He's an apiarist."

"Cool!" Collin pumped his fist in the air. Anna had no idea what Mr. Hoffman was talking about. Judging from the confused looks on all the other kids' faces, Anna wasn't the only one.

"Does anyone have a guess what an apiarist is?" Mr. Hoffman asked.

"Someone who studies apes!" Reed shouted. Then he jumped up, stuck his elbows out, and scratched his armpits, shouting, *"Ooh, ooh-ooh, ooh!"*

Most of the kids laughed, but Collin stretched his hand as high as it would go. If *he* knew what an apiarist was, then Anna knew it must have something to do with bugs. *Ugh.*

"Collin," Mr. Hoffman said, smiling at Anna's brother. "Why don't you tell us?"

"An apiarist is a beekeeper," Collin said.

"They have beehives full of honeybees."

"You are exactly right." Mr. Hoffman told everyone to split into pairs for the walk to the apiary. "It's only a couple blocks, but I want everyone to stay with their buddy." Mr. Hoffman leaned close to Anna and said in a low voice, "Would you be buddies with Collin today?"

Anna said yes, but inside her head she said, N-O F-A-I-R! She wanted to be buddies with Kaya, her best friend. Or maybe with Reed, another good friend. As they exited the Friendship Garden, Collin walked on his tip-toes, leaning forward, with his elbows tucked up and his hands dangling. "I'm a praying mantis," he told her.

Anna scowled. She hoped they didn't have to be partners for everything.

The apiary sat on the rooftop of a nearby apartment building. Anna and Collin and the rest of the Friendship Garden had to walk up four flights of stairs to get on the roof. Anna and Collin were last because Collin couldn't climb as fast as the bigger kids. When they finally walked out onto the roof, Anna saw lots of white, blue, and purple flowers growing in containers. On one side of the rooftop, a tall man with black hair, a white uniform, and a big screened helmet stood next to three tall, white wooden boxes that looked like they had lots of drawers. There were bees buzzing nearby.

Anna froze. She was afraid she might get stung. Collin let go of her hand and went to stand close to the white boxes with Mr. Hoffman and the two girls with pigtails, Clary and Abril. Anna stood farther back with the rest of the kids.

"I don't like bees," Reed whispered to Anna. "I've been stung four times!"

Kaya nodded. "I've never been stung, but

bees freak me out. I wish we were just gardening."

"Me too," Anna said out of the side of her mouth.

Mr. Blanco took off his screened hat and said, "Welcome to my wonderful world of bees."

He picked up a metal container that looked a little like a shiny silver watering can with smoke pouring out of the tip instead of water. "Honeybees are usually pretty gentle. A lot of people who think they are afraid of bees are really afraid of wasps. But this smoke will keep the bees very calm, so you don't have to stand so far back."

Mr. Blanco beckoned them forward. "*¡Ven aqui!* Come stand on the white line. You'll be safe."

Anna and the rest of her friends scooted up to the white line, but Anna still wasn't sure she liked the looks of the bees. Then Mr. Blanco asked, "Has anyone seen a beehive before?" He pried the lid off one of the tall, white boxes and pulled out a wooden frame filled with honeycomb. It was crawling with bees.

Anna couldn't take her eyes away from the small, fuzzy creatures scrambling over the perfect hexagons of honeycomb. If she forgot to think about their stingers, they were kind of cool.

"What are they doing?" Reed asked Mr. Blanco, pointing at the bees.

"Worker bees have many different jobs throughout their lives," Mr. Blanco explained. "They take care of the baby bees and also the queen bee, and they collect pollen and nectar from flowers. These bees are making wax to build new honeycomb and seal up the cells that are already full."

Mr. Blanco put the frame back into the hive, then covered the hive with the lid. "Does anyone know the two main ways honeybees help people?"

Kaya raised her hand. "Making honey *has* to be one of them, right?"

Mr. Blanco nodded. "*Si*. But who knows the other thing honeybees do?"

At first, no one raised a hand. Anna couldn't think of an answer. Besides making honey, the only other thing Anna knew that bees did was sting. That didn't seem like much help to people.

"If you like to garden, bees are really important!" Mr. Hoffman said.

Collin raised his hand. "Pollen!" he said.

"When bees visit flowers, they get pollen all over their legs. When they visit the next flower, they leave some pollen behind. Then the plant can grow fruit."

"Right!" said Mr. Blanco. "Follow me!" He beckoned them over to a group of flowers. Then he showed them how a flower had one part, the stamen, that was covered with pollen, and another part, the pistil, that would turn into seeds or fruit or nuts if the pollen could attach to it.

"Do *all* the plants in our garden need bees to grow?" Anna asked Mr. Hoffman.

"Not all of them," he explained.

"Did you know that honeybee colonies are dying?" Collin announced. Everyone got quiet and stared at him. Collin spread his arms, made a buzzing noise, and swooped around in a figure eight.

Anna felt a little embarrassed of her brother's buggy behavior, but Mr. Blanco nodded sadly. "He's right. And if we lose too many, that means lots of food that we enjoy— apples, blueberries, cucumbers, and more— might disappear."

Anna blinked. She couldn't believe what she was hearing. Apples, blueberries, and cucumbers? She ate those foods all the time. This was T-E-R-R-I-B-L-E!

Mr. Blanco led the group to an open-air tent on the other side of the roof. It was nice and shady, and everyone seemed excited when he gave them honey-sweetened lemonade and sheets of beeswax for making candles. But

Anna couldn't stop thinking about the honey-bees. She raised her hand.

"Why are the colonies dying?" she asked Mr. Blanco. "Can't we stop that from happening?"

Mr. Blanco shook his head. "It's a very complicated problem," he told Anna. "There are many reasons."

"Like pesticides," said Collin, scooting his chair near Anna's. "Also, bees don't have enough to eat. I'll tell you about it when we get home."

Anna turned back to her beeswax candle. She tucked the string for the wick inside and began to roll the sheet of beeswax. She tried to think about the flowers she would plant in the Friendship Garden that afternoon, but her mind kept picturing fuzzy little bees crawling all over the flowers.

"*Bzzz* Anna," Collin said, grabbing her arm. "*Bzzz* let's *bzzz* talk *bzzz* in Buzz language *bzzz* all *bzzz* day."

Anna rolled her eyes. She knew her brother was just trying to play with her, but he was so annoying sometimes! Buzz language? *All day?*

Suddenly Anna had a thought. "If we fix the bee problems, will they be okay?" Anna asked Mr. Blanco. She couldn't imagine living in a world where people couldn't grow food.

Mr. Blanco patted Anna's shoulder. "We should try," he told her. "If everyone pitched in, we might solve the problem."

Anna wanted to pitch in. She was *going* to help. Anna was determined. She would save the bees!

CHAPTER 3

ANNA TO THE RESCUE!

The next day at the Friendship Garden, Anna planted bright red geraniums with Kaya, Reed, and Collin. But she also kept her eyes on the lookout for bees. She couldn't help it. After their field trip, Anna had gone home and read all about bee colonies on the Internet.

"I don't see very many honeybees." Anna

felt a flutter of worry in her stomach as she glanced around the Friendship Garden. "Do you?"

Kaya rubbed the back of her hand across her forehead. "No, thank goodness. I don't want to get stung."

"But it's really wasps who are the main stingers," Anna said.

"Well, if I see any bees, I'm going to tell them to *buzz off*!" Reed folded his arms across his chest.

Just then, Collin zoomed toward them with arms outstretched like airplane wings. He made a buzzing noise and wore fuzzy

L-shaped antennae on his head.

"*Bzzz* hello," he said. "*Bzzz* I'm *bzzz* a *bzzz* bee!"

"Yeah?" said Reed. "Then you are the only bee in the world I like."

"Me too!" Kaya agreed.

Anna didn't agree.

"But bees are important, you guys." She pointed at the zucchini blossoms in their vegetable plot. "I never realized it before, but without bees, those flowers will never turn into big zucchinis."

Collin smiled at Anna. "Do you want me to make you your own antennae?"

"Um, no thanks," she told him.

"I don't even like zucchini," said Reed, digging the next hole.

"Me neither," Kaya agreed.

Anna threw her hands up in the air. "Don't you understand? It's not just zucchini. Tons of foods need bees to grow. Bees are *so* important."

Anna stood up. She couldn't get bees off her mind. But if her friends wouldn't listen to her, maybe the grown-ups would.

First, Anna walked over to Daisy's plot, near the front gate. Daisy was Kaya's grand-mother and sometimes helped Mr. Hoffman supervise the Friendship Garden after school. She was a really good gardener, but she wasn't like any other grandma Anna knew. Daisy had red curly hair and bright red lipstick and loved to kid around.

"*Hola*, Anna!" Daisy said when she saw Anna coming. "What can I do for you today? A cartwheel? A handspring? Or would you like me to yodel?"

"Maybe a little later." Anna chuckled. Then she got serious. "I can't stop thinking about bees."

Daisy looked all around her, then she tapped her finger against her lips, thinking. "You  know, I don't think I have noticed as many bees around this year." Daisy shook her head. "Strange."

Next, Anna went to visit Mr. Eggers's garden. He was the grumpiest member of Shoots and Leaves, but underneath all his grumpiness, he loved gardening and was always willing to help.

"Hello there, Anna," he said as he poured

one of his special homemade fertilizer mixes on his tomato plants. "The Friendship Garden is looking robust this year. Did you plant many pumpkins?"

"Lots," said Anna. "Did you know that bees pollinate pumpkins?"

Mr. Eggers looked surprised, then rubbed his mustache with two fingers and looked thoughtful. "Bees? I'll have to start paying more attention."

Anna nodded, then left to go talk with Maria, the garden president, who worked in a little shed by the entrance to the garden.

Along the way, she kept her eyes peeled for bees, but she only saw two.

She knocked on Maria's door. When Maria opened it, she gave Anna a great big smile.

"What's the project this time, Anna?" she said, laughing. "I know whenever you come to visit you've got an *idea*."

Anna shook her head. "I've just been thinking about bees," Anna told her.

Maria nodded and said, "Okay, I'm listening."

"They are really important."

Maria nodded. "They sure are."

"Did you know pesticides make bees so confused they can't find their hives?"

Maria shook her head.

"Maybe you should make a rule that no one is allowed to use pesticides anymore. Also, Shoots and Leaves should plant more wildflowers all around the garden. Wild-flowers attract bees. "

"Those are good ideas," Maria said. "But I'll have to check the budget to see if we have money to purchase the flowers, and I can't change a garden rule without a vote."

"Oh," said Anna. She was surprised Maria didn't want to help the bees. "I could help plant the flowers," Anna said.

"Thanks," Maria said. "I'll let you know, but I've got to get back to work now, okay?"

"Okay." Anna sighed as Maria closed the door to her shed. Anna stood there for a second more, her feet as heavy as rocks. Then Anna trudged back to the Friendship Garden.

"Where'd you go?" Reed handed Anna a pair of garden shears. "Mr. Hoffman said we could start harvesting the garlic scapes."

"I was just taking a walk," Anna told them, "and I got an idea. I'm going to save the bees! We should ask Mr. Hoffman if we can make all the rest of our flowers wildflowers."

"I like wildflowers," Kaya agreed, "but it's not like planting them in *one* garden is going to save the bees."

"Yeah." Reed snipped another scape. "Mr. Blanco said honeybee colonies are collapsing all over the *world*."

Anna's heart sank. Kaya and Reed were right. Making the Friendship Garden more bee-friendly was a start, but it wasn't enough to save all the bees.

"These are the cutest plants," Kaya said, twirling a curly green stem. "They remind me of pig's tails, only green."

Anna took her scissors and cut her own

scape as low as she could without damaging the leaves. Then she put the twisty green stalk in the basket sitting next to

Collin. He rubbed his leg against Anna's. "I'm transferring pollen to you."

Anna bit her lip. She didn't want to be mean, but her little brother wouldn't leave her alone! And it was keeping Anna from figuring out how to save the bees.

Collin smiled and cut another garlic scape. "Look," he said, pointing toward the tomato plants with his scape. "There's a bee."

Anna looked, but the bug she saw didn't look anything like a bee. "That's just a fly," she told Collin.

"Nuh-uh. There are lots more kinds of bees than honeybees," he said. "Honeybees are just the ones that beekeepers raise."

Maybe Collin was right, but Anna didn't have time to learn about other kinds of bees. Honeybees were her bees, and she wouldn't stop thinking about them until they, and all the fruits and vegetables Anna loved, were safe. Anna to the R-E-S-C-U-E!

CHAPTER 4

BEE-ING BRAVE

That afternoon, after Anna and Collin's father walked them home from the Friendship Garden, they found a notice tucked into the frame of their front door. It said:

LET'S KEEP OUR BLOCK BEAUTIFUL!
Please come to a neighborhood meeting
to discuss weeds and unruly lawns.
Tonight at 7:30 p.m.

"Anna," Collin said, tapping Anna's shoulder with his antennae, "want to see my bee book?"

Anna didn't have time to look at a little kid's book. She had work to do! "Maybe later," she told Collin, then turned to her father. "What do you think they meant by 'discuss weeds and unruly lawns'?" she asked.

Anna's father headed toward the laundry room and said, "Well, the meeting could be about the O'Malleys' house, you know, the one where they don't mow the lawn and the yard is covered with two feet of grass and Queen Anne's lace. I've heard a lot of neighbors complain that it's attracting all kinds of bugs and animals."

"Like bees?" Anna said, as she helped her dad lift the laundry out of the dryer and into the laundry basket.

"Sure, bees and other things, too. But the meeting might be about the dandelions, clover, and creeping Charlie all over *everyone's* lawns. If the whole block doesn't look nice, it can make all the houses less valuable." Anna's father carried the basket of laundry over to the sofa and began to fold it. Anna watched him with a queasy feeling. She was worried about this meeting.

"But what do they want to do about the weeds?" Anna asked, walking over to the couch and sitting next to her dad.

Mr. Fincher shrugged, and began to fold Anna's WORLD PEAS T-shirt. "My guess is that they want us to spray weed killer. That way all the weeds will go away and our lawns will look perfect."

Weed killer? A lot of those weeds were actually honeybee food. Maybe *this* was the way Anna could save the bees.

"Can I go to the meeting?" Anna asked her father.

He put down Collin's praying mantis T-shirt and stared at her like she had just asked to fly to the moon. "You want to go to a neighborhood meeting?" he asked. "Even Mommy and I never want to go. They're pretty boring."

Anna would face boring if it meant saving the bees. "I definitely want to go," she said.

"Okay then, I'll see if I can find a babysitter for Collin."

Anna and her father walked into the Lewis's house for the neighborhood meeting at seven thirty on the dot, but their living room was already crammed with people. The sofas and chairs even had grown-ups sitting on the arms, with more people standing behind them. Anna and her dad stood right inside the doorway since there wasn't really any other place to stand. Anna's stomach wobbled and her knees shook a little bit. She hadn't realized there would be so many people. Or that she would be the only kid.

"Thanks for coming, everyone," Mr. Lewis said, smiling. He had big muscles, deep brown skin, and a shiny bald head. "This should be a pretty quick meeting. I met with the guy from SprayGreen Lawn company and he said he'd give us a discount for doing the whole block. Any comments or questions before we vote on it?"

Anna opened her mouth, but then she

closed it again. Could she really do it? Talk to all those grown-ups by herself?

A burly man with reddish brown hair stood up and said, "I want to remind everyone that we *all* need to spray. I don't want to waste my money clearing my own yard, only to have seeds blow over from some clown down the street."

A bunch of people nodded, and Anna felt her throat tighten. What if everyone got angry at her for saying they shouldn't use weed killer?

"Any other comments?" Mr. Lewis looked around the room. "Okay then, let's vote." Mr. Lewis started to pass out paper and pencils.

"Wait!" Anna shouted, stepping forward. She was so nervous her knees were shaking. "You can't get rid of all the weeds and wild-flowers. The bees will starve without them."

A man on the opposite side of the room

snorted. "Who wants bees? We should spray to get rid of them too."

"No!" Anna said. "Please listen. Honeybees are really important. Without them, we couldn't grow a lot of our food. And they are in trouble. One of the ways we can help is by letting weeds and wildflowers like dandelions and clover grow in our yards."

When Anna finished talking, her heart was pounding, and the room was buzzing with everyone talking at once. Anna had never spoken to a big group of grown-ups like that. It was S-C-A-R-Y. But not as scary as a world without bees. Anna's father leaned down and whispered, "Way to go. I'm proud of you, Banana." Anna's heart slowed a little after that.

Mr. Lewis tried to settle everyone down. "One at time, people. Let's try to talk one at a time. Gina, you go first."

"I think we need to learn more about what Anna is telling us. I don't want to spray until I have all the facts."

"The *main* fact is that our street looks like a wild kingdom," shouted a man with glasses and a thick beard. "And my kid got stung in front of the O'Malley house just last week."

"It's a free country. He's allowed to let his lawn grow if he wants," yelled a tall, skinny woman who reminded Anna of a green bean.

Mr. Lewis tried to get everyone's attention again, but every time it seemed like the shouting was winding down, someone would start it back up again. After an hour, they still hadn't made a decision, and Anna's dad said it was time to go home and get ready for bed.

"But what if we leave and then everyone

decides to spray the weed killer? Can't we stay a little longer?" Anna pleaded.

Her father shook his head. "I have a feeling this could go on all night. The babysitter needs to get home and you have to wake up early for camp tomorrow. Sorry. But you got your message out there. That's important."

Anna dragged her feet as she and her father crossed the street back to their own house. She had hoped she would change everyone's minds and be done with it. Saving the bees was going to take forever!

LEMONADE FOR SALE!

The next day after camp, Reed and Kaya came home with Collin and Anna. Mr. Fincher made a yummy snack of apples with almond butter and honey.

"Did you know we wouldn't have this snack without bees?" Anna asked her friends.

They just shrugged, but Collin said, "Yeah! They need millions and millions of bees! Each bee only makes a pea-size drop of honey in its *entire* life."

Anna watched Reed and Kaya give each other a look. She thought that maybe they didn't want to hang out with Collin anymore. Today he was wearing not only his bee antenna, but two giant bee eyes on his forehead, a yellow-and-black striped shirt, and iridescent bee wings.

"We're going outside to play in the sprinklers, okay, Dad?" Anna said.

"Sure." He cleared their plates. "Take Collin with you, though, since I have to do the vacuuming."

Anna groaned on the inside and hoped her friends wouldn't be too upset. But Reed jumped up from the table and shouted, "Last one in their bathing suit is a rotten banana!"

Outside, Anna made up a really fun game called Trickle, Trickle, Spray! One person closed their eyes and kinked the hose while everyone else kept running through the dry sprinkler. Then the hose person would let the

water go again, and whoever was closest to the sprinkler got soaked. That person became the next hose holder. After a while, though, everyone was ready to do something else.

"Let's have a lemonade stand," Anna suggested.

"I'll make the signs," Kaya said. She was a really good artist.

"I'll test the lemonade to make sure it tastes good," Reed said. "That's a really important job."

"You can test it a little bit, but not too much, or we won't have anything to sell," Anna told Reed.

"Can I help?" Collin asked.

Anna bit her lip. Now that they were dried off, he was back in his bee costume. And he was carrying his magnifying glass, butterfly net, and a giant insect encyclopedia. "Look! A cicada shell." Collin grabbed the old empty skin of a cicada off the oak tree in their yard

and held it right under Anna's nose. Anna leaned back. G-R-O-S-S!

"Sorry, all the jobs are taken," Anna explained. "Kaya's making the signs. Reed's testing the lemonade, and I'm making it. I'm going to use Mom's recipe for lemonade with honey."

Collin's shoulders sank. His head drooped. "Oh," he said. "Okay."

Anna got a guilty feeling in her stomach.

She didn't want Collin to feel bad. She wished he would just go hunt for grasshoppers or something.

"I guess you could help me stir the lemonade," she said.

Collin's face turned into a beam of sunshine. "I'm really good at stirring!"

When everything was ready for the lemonade stand, Collin, Anna, Reed, and Kaya set up a little table on the sidewalk in front of Anna's house. They taped Kaya's sign, a drawing of a lemon tree growing glasses of lemonade instead of lemons, on the front of the table. The sign said: LEMONADE, 50¢

Then they sat in little chairs behind the table and waited. And waited. There was no one on their block. It was a little bit B-O-R-I-N-G. Kaya was drawing another picture, Reed was

testing another cup of lemonade, and Collin was studying an ant hill, when a small truck finally turned onto their street.

"Get ready," Anna said, and they all stood up.

As the truck drove closer, they shouted, "Lemonade! Buy some lemonade!" The truck didn't stop. It didn't even slow down. But when Anna saw the side of the truck, she didn't want it to stop. It was a SprayGreen Lawn truck. Anna hoped it wasn't driving down her street because the neighbors hadn't listened to her. Her father told her they hadn't taken a vote yet. They were going to have another meeting.

Suddenly Anna couldn't believe she was just sitting around not selling lemonade. She shouldn't be lazing away her days while the bees were still in trouble. She had to do something, but what?

"I just had the best idea!" Anna told Kaya and Reed.

"What?" they said.

"Instead of having a lemonade stand, we should put all our supplies in a wagon and go door to door."

Reed stood up, ready to get the wagon.

"You're right. We'll sell tons more lemonade that way."

Anna shook her head. "I don't think we should sell it!" Her hands felt all fluttery with excitement. *This* was how she could save the bees. "We should give it away for free. When people realize how delicious it is, we can tell them that if it wasn't for bees, we wouldn't have such a yummy drink. Then we can tell them all about how bee colonies are collapsing and how they need to plant wildflowers and let their weeds grow, and . . ."

Anna stopped. She noticed Kaya and Reed looking at each other again.

"What?" she asked. "You don't want to?"

Kaya sighed. "It's not that," she said. "I know bees are important. But it feels like ever since our field trip, all you ever talk about is bees."

"It's not *all* I ever talk about." Anna didn't understand why her friends couldn't see what a good idea this was. "You guys *never* want to talk about bees."

"I want to talk about bees," Collin said. *"Bzzz buzz buzzbuzz bzzz."*

Anna rubbed her palms against her forehead. Collin was always interrupting everything.

"We *do* want to talk about bees," Reed said, his voice growing louder with each word. "Just not all the time. We're kids. We want to have fun too."

"Sorry," Kaya said, putting her hand on Anna's arm. "But it makes me too sad to think about it all the time the way you do. I want to help, but there's really not that much we can do."

Anna felt like a wilted daisy. Ever since she first moved to Chicago and started her new school, she and Kaya and Reed had helped each other out with everything. They'd been partners and best friends. When Anna wanted a place to make friends and plant things, Reed and Kaya had helped her start the Friendship Garden. When Reed wanted to win a pumpkin contest, Anna and Kaya cheered him on. When Kaya wanted a pet, Reed and Anna helped build a chicken coop. They were supposed to be F-R-I-E-N-D-S!

But now, when Anna wanted to save the bees, Reed and Kaya wanted . . .

Anna didn't know what they wanted. But she knew what they didn't want. They didn't want to help. Anna was on her own. They spent the rest of the afternoon sitting quietly at their lemonade stand, selling only four cups of lemonade. Anna planned to use her fifty cents to buy wildflower seeds for her backyard, but it wasn't enough. And if Anna couldn't find anyone else who cared about the bees the way she did, she didn't know if she could ever do enough.

That night at bedtime, Collin said, "Anna, do you want to read my bee book with me *now*?"

Anna shook her head, "Sorry, Collin. Not now." Learning that bees have five eyes and four wings, or that they do a waggle dance, wasn't going to help her convince more people to care. Maybe Kaya and Reed were right. Maybe it was just too big a job.

Anna watered her three houseplants, Chloe, Fern, and Spike, and blew them a kiss good night. At least they'd be fine even if all the bees disappeared.

CHAPTER 6

MMMM, HONEY!

Anna loved Saturday mornings, because if she woke up early enough, her mom would let her come to the farmers' market to buy fruits and vegetables for the restaurant. Just the two of them. It was one of the best times of the week. Anna loved seeing all the stalls bursting with different shapes and colors, red bell peppers, yellow squash, purple kale, and orange carrots. She'd been so busy thinking about bees, she almost forgot how much she loved the market.

As they walked from farmer to farmer, Anna and her mom passed a booth selling garlic scapes. "Hey! We just picked those at the Friendship Garden!"

Anna's mother picked up a bunch and smelled them. "Mmm," she said, "these would be great in a salad dressing." She told the farmer to send a carton to her restaurant.

Next Anna and her mother went to a booth with all different kinds of lettuce. There were so many different shades of green, from light yellow-green to dark, dark blackish-green. It reminded Anna of a green rainbow. *A greenbow*, Anna thought, chuckling to herself. She loved naming things.

While her mother inspected different heads of lettuce, Anna let her eyes roam around the market. In addition to people selling fruits and vegetables, there were also cheesemakers, bakers, and people who made fancy jellies and jams. At the very edge of the market, Anna noticed a tiny booth she hadn't seen there before.

Anna squinted her eyes to be sure she was seeing correctly. She was. The person at the booth was Mr. Blanco. A beekeeper at the farmers' market? Of course! Honeybees and gardens went together.

"Mom," she said, tugging her mother's elbow. "There's the beekeeper I was telling you about. Can we go see him?"

Her mother ripped off a tiny piece of watercress and took a bite. "I'll take three bunches," she told the farmer. Then she turned to Anna.

"Sweetie, I'm not done with my shopping, but if you want to walk down there, you can. Just make sure you stay where we can see each other."

"Okay," Anna said. She really wanted her mother to meet Mr. Blanco, but she knew her mother had to finish shopping first. "It's the table with the honeybee sign, all the way at the end."

Anna wove through the customers until she reached Mr. Blanco's booth. "Hi," she said. "Remember me? I'm Anna. My summer camp just did a field trip to your roof."

"Anna!" Mr. Blanco shook Anna's hand. "I remember you. I'm so glad you found me here. This is my first week selling honey at the farmers' market."

Anna looked at the stacks of round glass

jars filled with golden liquid.
Mmmm, H-O-N-E-Y!

A row of jars at the front
of the table made another
kind of rainbow.
Some of them were
light and clear all
the way down to a
deep red.

"These are my
flavored honeys."

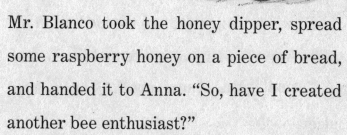

Mr. Blanco took the honey dipper, spread
some raspberry honey on a piece of bread,
and handed it to Anna. "So, have I created
another bee enthusiast?"

Anna nodded and took a bite of the sample.
It tasted sweet and tart and rich all at once.
And the yummy taste lingered on her tongue.

"I've been trying to save the bees," Anna told Mr. Blanco, taking another bite. Maybe he could tell her what to do.

"That's wonderful," he said. "The more people who learn what's happening, and the more people who care, the better."

Anna looked at the stack of wooden honey dippers in a bowl next to the honey. She shifted the bowl to the right. "But that's the problem. It seems like I can't get anyone to care!"

"Excuse me a moment," Mr. Blanco said to Anna, when two customers stepped up to his table. Anna took another bite and listened as he told the man and woman all about his local honey.

"It tastes delicious because my bees visit so many different kinds of flowers. I also make flavored honey." He lifted a honey dipper from a jar with a yellow ribbon and spread honey on two small squares of bread. "Try some lemon honey," he said, handing them the samples.

The couple took their bites and the woman closed her eyes as she chewed. "Delicious!" she said. "We'll take a jar."

The woman paid Mr. Blanco and took her honey. Then she and the man walked off.

"How did you learn to be a beekeeper?" Anna asked when it was just the two of them again.

"My grandfather was an apiarist and my mother, too." Mr. Blanco made himself a sample and popped the whole thing into his mouth. "It's something I've been doing since I was a boy. But when I moved to the city, I thought I might have to give it up."

"Yeah," Anna said. "It seems like bees are more of a country thing."

Mr. Blanco nodded. "But my bees are really happy in Chicago. As long as there are enough parks and gardens and flowers. Let me show you some more stuff."

Mr. Blanco reached under the table and brought out a jar of honeycomb, a couple of plastic replicas of bees, and more sheets of beeswax. As he began to tell Anna about all the different body parts of bees, more and more people gathered around the table, including Anna's mother.

"Mom!" Anna couldn't wait for her mom to try a sample. "You should use Mr. Blanco's honey in your restaurant, it's so good."

Mr. Blanco handed Anna's mother a sample, and she dipped her pinky in the honey and took a taste. Her eye's widened. "The flavors are so complex," she said. "How much?"

When Mr. Blanco told her the price, Mrs. Fincher's mouth twisted into a frown. "Unfortunately, it's too expensive for me to buy for the restaurant, but I will take two jars for myself. One lemon honey and one jalapeño honey."

As Anna's mom reached into her purse for the money, Anna leaned over and whispered, "You're in charge. Can't you make the restaurant buy Mr. Blanco's honey? It helps the bees."

Mrs. Fincher shook her head sadly. "If I spend all my money on honey, sweetie, I won't have enough left to buy the other ingredients I need. At least we'll get to eat all this deliciousness at home!"

Before they left, Anna's mother took Mr. Blanco's business card and said thank you.

Then they squeezed past the crowd of people waiting for a honey sample and went home.

That afternoon, Anna lay on the couch staring at the ceiling. She wanted to call Kaya and Reed, but they didn't want to hear about bees anymore, and she didn't know if she could go a whole afternoon without talking about them.

Collin sat down next to Anna's head and leaned his face over hers. He looked upside

down to Anna. "I've got my bee book," he said. "It's really good."

Anna sighed and said, "Fine." She didn't want to read a little kid's book, but she didn't have anything better to do.

Collin opened the book and cleared his throat. "Have you ever wondered why bees buzz?"

Anna tilted her head. She hadn't wondered before, but now she was curious. Why did bees buzz?

"There are many different reasons," Collin continued. "Bees buzz when they fly and their wings vibrate. They also buzz when their nests are attacked and when they are shaking pollen from a flower."

Collin turned the page. "Want to hear another one?"

Anna sat up. She couldn't believe it, but now she did kind of want to hear another one.

"What do bees eat?" Collin read. "Honeybees eat nectar and pollen from flowers, but their babies, or larva, eat honey. Queen Bees eat royal jelly."

The more Collin read, the more Anna realized his book was actually filled with cool and interesting information. She didn't know there were more than four thousand different kinds of bees in America or that some bees live in mud instead of hives.

But when Collin got to the last page, Anna couldn't believe her ears.

"There are five things that kids can do to help honeybees," Collin said. Anna scooted closer to look at the book over his shoulder. She read the list as fast as she could.

1) Plant wildflowers and bee-friendly plants

2) Let weeds grow

3) Stay calm when you see a bee and don't destroy its home

4) Buy local honey

5) Spread the word so that others can help the bees too

Anna turned to Collin, "I'm already doing one through four," she said, "but I'm trying to do number five and it's not working. No one wants to learn about what's happening to bees. They think it's too boring or sad or dumb."

"I don't think it's those things," Collin said. "I promise I will never use any weed killers."

Anna smiled. "Thanks," she said. "But it seems like everyone else I talk to ignores me."

Kaya, Reed, her neighbors. Even her mom, who wouldn't buy Mr. Blanco's honey for her restaurant.

"Yeah." Collin sighed. "It's too bad you can't make it really fun, like our field trip."

Suddenly Anna froze. She couldn't believe it, but Collin had actually given her an idea. "Maybe it *can* be fun!"

Bees were cool. Anna liked the field trip and visiting Mr. Blanco's booth at the fair. She even liked reading the bee book. Kaya and Reed liked eating foods with honey. And the neighbors sure liked meetings. Maybe she could combine all those things.

"What if I throw a party?" Anna wondered out loud. "I could call it a Bee Bash. And we could serve food made with honey, and every-one could plant wildflowers, and I could make up a game: Pin the Pollen on the Flower!"

Anna jumped up. She couldn't wait to ask her parents if she could host a Bee Bash.

"Anna!" Collin called out, chasing her down the hall. "Can I help?"

Anna stopped and looked at her brother. He could be a little annoying sometimes, but he was also the only one who seemed to care about bees. Sometimes, he even had some good ideas. Maybe he wasn't actually *that* bad.

"Okay," Anna said, giving Collin a fist bump. "Let's do it!"

THE BIG
BEE BASH

Anna and Collin spent all of Sunday afternoon making special invitations for the Bee Bash. They folded a sheet of yellow construction paper in half and added black stripes. On the yellow stripes they wrote, *Please come to our Bee Bash*. Then on the inside of the card, they wrote:

Come to Anna and Collin's house
for honey-sweetened treats,
waggle dancing, and bee games
and activities.

Monday night at 7 p.m.

When all the invitations were finished, they took a walk all around their neighborhood with their mom and dad and passed out invitations to their friends and neighbors. They brought an invitation to Mr. Blanco, and Anna showed her parents his hives. Anna asked him to bring his cool bee stuff and honey to sell. She knew *he* could get people excited about bees.

Last, they went to Shoots and Leaves and posted the invitation on the bulletin board. Then Anna posted a sign she had made.

WILDFLOWER FUND

If you would like to help Shoots and Leaves attract more bees, please donate in the can below.

Anna shook her can before setting it on the bench below the bulletin board. It was empty to start, but hopefully that would change after the Bee Bash.

The next day at the Friendship Garden summer program, Maria, Daisy, Mr. Eggers, Mr. Hoffman, and all the kids told her they would come.

"I can't wait to learn how to waggle dance," Reed said, shaking his bottom.

"Who's making the food?" Kaya asked. "Your mom or your dad?" Sometimes Anna's father made really crazy recipes, like cocoa mushroom fritters and watermelon and mint pizza.

"They are both cooking," Anna told her. "And I picked all the recipes." The food would use Mr. Blanco's honey. "It's going to be yummy. I promise."

For the rest of the day, everyone was talking about the Bee Bash.

That night after dinner, Anna set a big jug of honey-sweetened lemonade on a table in the backyard. Collin carried out a tray of lemon-honey cupcakes, and Anna's mother packed a cooler full of homemade honey-cinnamon ice cream. Mr. Fincher was in charge of the deco-rations, big bouquets of wildflowers and black-and-yellow striped balloons. When Mr. Blanco arrived, he set up a table where guests could

make their own beeswax candles and he could tell people about his honey. Finally, everything was ready.

Kaya and Reed arrived first, and they tested out Anna's Pin the Pollen on the Flower game. Anna put a blindfold on Reed, spun him around, then laughed when he tried to stick the yellow circle of pollen on Kaya's nose.

"You wouldn't make a very good bee." Kaya laughed as she steered Reed in the direction of the apple blossom poster Anna had made. Reed stuck his pollen on the branch.

"I guess that blossom won't be turning into an apple this time," Anna told him.

"No fair!" Reed said, peeking to see where he'd stuck the pollen. "Bees don't have to wear blindfolds!"

Next, Anna taught Kaya and Reed how to do a waggle dance. She showed them the figure-eight footprints she drew in chalk on the patio to teach the pattern of the dance. "You have to shake your stomach when you're in the middle." Anna demonstrated with a big belly jiggle. Then she noticed some of the

grown-ups from the neighborhood meeting arriving with their kids. "I'll be right back," she told Kaya and Reed, and left to greet her new guests.

"Would you like to plant some wildflowers?" Anna asked.

Everyone wanted to, so Anna led them to the corner of her backyard, where her father said she could have her own wildflower garden. She showed them where to dig and how deep to plant, then left them to have fun in the dirt. She even heard one woman say, "We should plant a wildflower patch by our mailbox."

Anna grabbed a honey-cinnamon ice cream and took a bite as she looked around the Bee Bash. The mix of cool and creamy, sweet and spicy, spread over her tongue as she watched people reading bee books, waggle dancing, and making candles. A warm feeling spread across her chest. Maybe she had finally done it. Maybe now everything would change. And this was just the start!

Just as she was licking the last drops of her ice cream, Anna spotted Collin out of the corner of her eye. He was spinning in figure eights and buzzing like a bee. He was also V-E-R-Y close to Mr. Blanco's bee table. Mr. Blanco wasn't there, but his stack of honey jars were.

CRASH. Before she could stop him, Collin knocked right into the table!

"Collin! No!"

The pyramid jiggled but didn't fall over. Anna ran over and steadied the table. She breathed a sigh of relief. "You have to be careful! You could have made a sticky mess. Or ruined our Bee Bash." She shook her finger in Collin's face.

Collin hung his head. "Oh," he said softly. "I'm sorry."

Anna felt terrible. She knew her brother

didn't mean to make trouble. She kneeled down in front of Collin.

"It's okay," she said.

Collin smiled. "But the Bee Bash is a big success!" He pointed around at all the people having fun.

Anna nodded. She closed her eyes as she imagined all that she could do. Anna could host more and more Bee Bashes. She could outlaw pesticides and weed killers everywhere. She could make farmers plant lots of different kinds of plants instead of just one so that bees would have a variety of foods. She could convince people to start hives all over the country. She could cover the whole world with wildflowers! Anna's thoughts swarmed with possibilities.

When the sky turned pink and dusky,

everyone began to pack up and go home. Anna handed each guest a party favor filled with wildflower seeds and a list of the top five things they could do to help honeybees.

When Kaya and Reed said good night, Anna said, "I'm sorry all I've been talking about lately is bees. I just really care about them."

"We understand." Kaya gave Anna a hug. "We care about them too. And we care about you!"

"And we like having fun!" Reed said. "I'm going to tell my mom that I want to have a Bee Bash too."

"And my mom is going to use Mr. Blanco's honey as a topping at our FroYo store," Kaya said.

"Mmmm," Anna said.

That night, when Anna went to sleep, her

brain danced with thoughts of the neighbor-hood meeting. The new vote would take place the next day. Anna hoped she'd convinced everyone that bees were more important than perfect lawns.

The next day at the Friendship Garden, the vote was still at the front of her mind. Anna even had a hard time concentrating on her job of watering the plants. She wondered if there would be any discussion first, if she would be allowed to give one last speech about the bees, or if people were sick of thinking about it already. She was so absorbed in her thoughts that she lost track of what she was doing and watered Maria's shoe.

"Whoa!" Maria jumped back out of the way.

"Sorry," Anna said, trying not to smile when she saw Kaya and Reed giggling behind

Maria's back. "I was daydreaming."

"That's okay," Maria said. "That's why I wear rubber shoes. I just came over to tell you how your Bee Bash affected Shoots and Leaves."

Anna raised her eyebrows, and let a half smile spread across her face.

Maria smiled back. "A lot of our members want to stop using pesticides."

"Yes!" Anna pumped her fist in the air. Her party had worked! Now she couldn't wait for the neighborhood meeting.

That night, Anna and her father walked across the street to Mr. Lewis's house one more time. Anna couldn't believe it, but she thought it might be even more crowded than it was before. She and her father had to stand in the hallway outside of the living room.

"Thanks for coming, everyone," Mr. Lewis said. "I think we've all gotten a chance to discuss this enough, so we are going to get right to the vote. I know none of us want to stay as late as last week."

Mr. Lewis handed out strips of paper to all the grown-ups. He didn't hand one to Anna. "Sorry, kid," he said. "Only homeowners get to vote."

Mr. Fincher gave Anna his paper. "You can write our family's vote," he said.

Mr. Lewis cleared his throat. "Okay, listen up. I don't want anyone voting the wrong way by accident. If you want to spray for weeds, write yes; if you don't, write no, it's as simple as that. When you're finished, come put your paper in this bowl. We'll count the votes right away. We'll need a three-fourths majority for a decision."

Anna opened her slip of paper and wrote N-O! in all capital letters with an exclamation mark. She threaded her way through the crowd and put her paper in the bowl. Then she stayed close to the front to watch what happened. When everyone's vote was cast, Anna watched as Mr. Lewis read each slip and then made a tally mark on a piece of paper. It felt like it took forever, but finally he stood up and said, "The vote is in, and we have a three-fourths majority."

Anna felt tingles all over her body. She knew she'd won. There was no way everyone would spray weed killer after all that she'd done.

"The majority rules, and the decision is that we *will* hire SprayGreen Lawn company. I'll give Larry a call and set something up for next week."

Anna's chest felt like it had a crater the size of a watermelon. Her ears were ringing and her eyes prickled. They were going to spray. After everything she did. It wasn't enough. Suddenly the room felt like it was shrinking and the crowd felt like it was growing. Anna's eyes burned and watered. She turned and wove her way back to her father.

He tilted his head to the side and puckered the center of his brow. "I'm sorry, Anna. It was a good try."

Anna felt a tear, hot and heavy, ready to

slip from her eye. She didn't want to cry in front of all her neighbors, so she said, "Can we go home now?"

Her father rubbed her back and nodded, and they slipped out of the meeting without saying good-bye.

SWEET ENDINGS

When Anna got home, she went straight to her room. First, she watered her plants, and second, she lay down on her bed and cried. She had tried so hard, but she failed. Anna's heart hurt when she thought about how the honeybees might really disappear, and how she couldn't stop it.

Anna heard a squeaky noise behind her, so

she sat up and saw her parents walk into her room. They each sat on the edge of her bed.

"It's really disappointing when you work hard for something and it doesn't go the way you want," her dad said. "You must feel sad."

Anna nodded. "And I feel dumb," she said, "for thinking I could actually do anything to help. One kid can't make a difference."

"But you *did* make a difference," Anna's mom said. "You made a difference at Shoots and Leaves, and you taught a lot of people about bees. That's how it is when we're trying to make the world a better place. It might be too big a job for one person to solve a huge problem all by themselves, but if every person does the little bit that they can, it will all add up."

Anna's father nodded. "You should feel

proud of what you've accomplished, Banana. I know I am."

Anna sniffed and gave her parents a hug. She swallowed the lump in her throat and said, "So do you think I should keep trying to help the bees?"

"Absolutely," her parents answered.

"But maybe I can do other stuff too, right? I don't have to help them all the time, even though they need lots of help?" Maybe Anna could be a honeybee person *and* a gardening person. And a person who liked to make up names and games. She could be lots of different things.

"Just listen to your heart," Anna's mom said. "It will tell you what's right. The bees need you, but so do your friends, and your family and yourself. You can make time in your life for all the things you love and care about."

Anna nodded. That sounded good.

"Say," said Anna's father. "It's not too late. What do you say we take a walk and get a little FroYo?"

"Sounds good to me!" said Collin, popping his head in at the door and making a clicking sound over and over again with the tiny metal clicker in his hand. "Crickets love FroYo, but they go on hops, not walks."

Everyone laughed, and Collin hopped over to Anna's bed to join them.

Anna didn't care if they went for a walk or a hop, as long as they ended up at Kaya's frozen yogurt shop. Anna was going to have hers topped with honey. Honey tasted just like summer. S-W-E-E-T!

❧

The next day, after Sweet Peas and Honey-bees, Anna and Collin walked to the gate of Shoots and Leaves expecting to see their dad. But it was their mom standing on the sidewalk waiting for them.

"What are you doing here?" Anna asked. "Did something happen at the restaurant?"

Anna's mother usually left for work just before lunch and stayed at the restaurant until after dinner, sometimes even after bedtime. She was almost never home in the middle of the afternoon.

"Did the restaurant close?" Collin asked. "Are we going to move back to New York?"

Mrs. Fincher laughed. "The restaurant didn't close. It's fine. It's better than fine, actually. Something very exciting is going to happen, and I thought you'd like to see."

"What?" Anna and Collin both asked at the same time.

Anna's mom smiled mysteriously. "It's a surprise."

Anna waved good-bye to Kaya, Reed, and Mr. Hoffman, and then she and Collin walked ten blocks, past clothing stores and bakeries, dentist's offices and a pet store, all the way to Lemongrass, their mom's restau-rant. When they got to the red-brick storefront with the black-and-white striped awning, Anna was surprised to Mr. Blanco standing in front.

"Miguel!" Anna's mother said, shaking

his hand. "I'm so glad you could meet us this afternoon."

"It's my pleasure," Mr. Blanco said. "Good to see you two again," he told Anna and Collin.

Anna gasped and grabbed her mother's hand. "Mom! Did you decide to use Mr. Blanco's honey?" She started jumping around and doing a happy dance, and Collin joined her. The grown-ups laughed.

"I'm not ordering Mr. Blanco's honey, you silly-billies," Anna's mom said.

Anna looked up at her mom, confused. She'd been so excited about her mom using the honey, it was stinky to find out it wasn't true. But her mother had a twinkle in her eye and a smile tugging at the corner of her mouth.

"It's something even better. Come see."

Mrs. Fincher led Anna, Collin, and Mr.

Blanco through the dining room of the restaurant filled with tables covered in crisp white tablecloths and bouquets of sunny yellow flowers. They followed her through the gleaming stainless steel kitchen where everything shone like mirrors. Finally, she led them out the back door to a set of wooden stairs that led up to the roof.

The roof! Anna's heart began to flutter and shake, like it was doing a happy dance of its own. She thought she might know what her mother was going to show her, but she didn't even want to think it until she was sure.

"Why are we going to the roof?" Collin asked. "Are there going to be bees up there?"

Anna held her breath and they reached the top steps.

"Yes," said their mother, sweeping her

arms in front of them to show them the containers of wildflowers and the two tall, white boxes. "I knew I couldn't afford Mr. Blanco's honey, but I couldn't get the taste out of my mind, so I called some other chefs I know who have rooftop apiaries and they said it was about the same amount of work as taking care of a cat."

"I can help you take care of them," Collin said. "I know a lot about bees."

"I'd love your help, both of you. Mr. Blanco is going to teach us everything we need to know."

"Why don't you put on these suits," Mr. Blanco said, handing everyone white coveralls with white helmets.

Anna and Collin both had to roll up the legs and the sleeves, the suits were so big. When

they were on, they put on their helmets and gloves too, and walked up close to the hives. Mr. Blanco puffed the smoker a couple times, then lifted the lid. He pulled out a frame, and Anna saw dozens of bees crawling over the top bar, but there wasn't very much honeycomb.

"They're just getting started," Mr. Blanco said. "Hold out your hand."

Anna did what he told her. He put his finger up close to a hive and a fuzzy little bee landed on it. He gently brought his finger close to Anna and let the bee crawl onto her glove. It's clear wings were so delicate and beautiful, but Anna almost had to laugh at the way its bottom kept pulsing up and down, like it was keeping the beat to a song only the bee could hear. Its long black antennae twitched.

It was such a teeny-tiny creature, Anna thought, but it was so important. Well, not all by itself. One bee couldn't pollinate all the crops on the planet, but all the bees working together could. Anna realized she was just like the bee. All by herself she couldn't save them, but with a whole hive of people, she got rid of the pesticides at Shoots and Leaves, planted a bunch of wildflowers, convinced her mom to start two new colonies, and taught lots and lots of people about bees. If all those people started their own helper hives, soon there *would* be enough people to save the bees.

The honeybee crawled along the edge of Anna's finger, then flew back to its hive.

"Work hard, little bee," she whispered. "I will too!"

ACTIVITY: **THE WAGGLE DANCE GAME**

What you will need:

Paper, markers, and scissors

A room to play in

How to play:

1. Draw a picture of a flower and cut it out.

2. While your friends close their eyes, hide the flower somewhere in the room.

3. Next you have to tell your friends where the flower is without talking or pointing. You will use a waggle dance, just like a bee. A waggle dance is when a bee flies in a double loop pattern like the drawing on the next page.

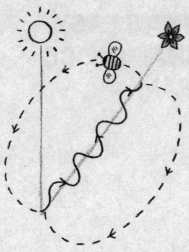

The bee uses the wiggly flight up the center of the double loop to give directions to the other bees. When a flower is close, the bee flies for a short distance up the center of the loops. When a flower is far, the bee flies for a longer distance. When a flower is to the left of the hive, the bee points the center line to the left, and when the flower is to the right, the bee flies toward the right.

4. After you've done your waggle dance, your friends can try to find your flower.

Good luck!

RECIPE: **ANNA'S EASY HONEY CINNAMON ICE CREAM**

(serves 1)

Ingredients:

Ice cubes

1 cup half-and-half

$\frac{1}{2}$ cup kosher salt

1 tbsp. sugar

1 tbsp. honey

$\frac{1}{2}$ tsp. cinnamon

$\frac{1}{2}$ tsp. vanilla extract

1 pint-size Ziploc bag

1 gallon-size Ziploc bag

Instructions:

Combine the half-and-half, sugar, honey,

cinnamon, and vanilla extract in the pint-size bag. Seal the bag very carefully, so that none of the liquid will leak out. You might want to use two bags.

Fill the gallon-size Ziploc bag halfway with ice cubes, then sprinkle kosher salt over the ice cubes.

Next put the smaller bag filled with ingredients inside the bigger bag of ice and salt and seal the big bag.

Shake the two bags together for 5–10 minutes until the liquid mixture begins to turn to ice cream. You can check the small bag halfway through to see the consistency of your ice cream.

Once the ice cream isn't too runny anymore, scoop it into a bowl and enjoy!

Don't miss the next
FRIENDSHIP GARDEN
book, *Starry Skies and Fireflies*